MW00911441

Enchanted Stables

By Lara Bergen
Illustrated by the Disney Storybook Artists

New York

For information address Disney Press, 114 Fifth Avenue, New York, 10011-5690.

Printed in the United States of America

First Edition

1 3 5 7 9 10 8 6 4 2

Library of Congress Catalog Card Number on file

ISBN-13: 978-1-4231-0478-0

ISBN-10: 1-4231-0478-1

For more Disney Press fun, visit www.disneybooks.com

Table of Contents

Walt Disney's

Cinderella

The Heart of a Champion

Life at the palace was a dream come true for Cinderella, and she took care to share her good fortune with everyone she loved. This included her dear old horse, Frou, who had been her faithful friend since she was a child.

One day, Cinderella was visiting Frou in the royal stable when her mouse friends, Jaq and Gus, ran up to tell her that a messenger had arrived at the palace! Cinderella said good-bye to Frou and the other horses, and hurried off to hear the news.

Cinderella arrived at the castle just in time to hear the Grand Duke read the invitation aloud: "'Dear King—'" he began.

"That's me!" the King said, beaming.

"Quite so," the Grand Duke agreed. "Ahem. 'You and your family,'" he read on, "'are hereby invited to attend this year's annual Royal International Horse Show, to be held exactly one week from today. Please choose one member from your royal household to represent you in the competition.'"

"Whoopie!" exclaimed the King. "I love horse shows. Blue ribbon, here I come!"

"Er . . . you know, Your Majesty," the Grand Duke said, "every year you enter the competition . . . and every year you come in last. Perhaps, just this once, someone else should—"

"Silence!" cried the King. "I have an idea. Every year, *I* enter the competition. Perhaps, just this once, *someone else* should represent our kingdom."

"Brilliant, Your Majesty," the Grand Duke said. "I would never have thought of that."

17th

"You know, Father," the Prince spoke up, "there's no finer horsewoman in the kingdom than Cinderella. I think *she* should represent us."

"Cinderella?" the King said in surprise. He rubbed his chin thoughtfully, then he smiled.

"That," he declared, "is an excellent idea!"

The next thing Cinderella knew, the King was leading her out of the palace and back to the royal stable.

"Naturally," he told Cinderella, his voice echoing across the stalls, "the finest horsewoman in the kingdom must have the finest *horse* in the kingdom. I have a stable full of champions, my dear. We'll choose the best of the best, and you can begin training right away. Ah, yes! I can see those blue ribbons already!"

The King ordered his groomsmen to saddle up his fanciest horses—all one hundred and twenty-two of them—and bring them out to the courtyard for Cinderella to see. Within minutes, there was a row of regal steeds lined up as far as the eye could see.

"Come, Cinderella," the King said, pointing toward the first horse. "Climb on. Don't be shy. You can't know if the shoe fits unless you try it on!"

Cinderella climbed onto the back of the first horse. She knew this stallion was one of the King's personal favorites.

But he was just a bit too small.

"Too bad," said the King, shaking his head. "Next!"

The next horse, however, was too *big*. . . .

The one after that wasn't quite right either. . . .

And neither was the next one. . . .

Or the next one!

Finally, Cinderella slid down from the saddle of a nervous Thoroughbred and dashed back into the stable.

"I'll be right back!" she called to the King, the Prince, and the Grand Duke. "I know the perfect horse! You'll see!"

Moments later, Cinderella returned, leading Frou! The old horse was a bit bewildered to find himself on display before the King.

The King stared at Cinderella and Frou in disbelief.

"What's this?" he demanded.

"Why, 'this' is a horse!" Cinderella replied with a laugh. She rubbed Frou's shaggy mane. "The best horse in the kingdom, in fact!"

"My dear," said the King, turning up his nose. "If none of my horses suits your fancy, I can have another hundred champions here by morning!"

"Frou may be old," said Cinderella, "but he has the heart of a champion!"

And with that, she saddled Frou and swung herself up.

"Come on, Frou," she told him. "Let's show them what you've got."

But the first thing Frou did was trip over a nearby water trough. Cinderella flew over Frou's head. She landed in the trough with a *splash*! The other horses whinnied with laughter. Frou hung his head.

"Don't worry," Cinderella said to the King, as well as to Frou. "By next week, we'll be ready."

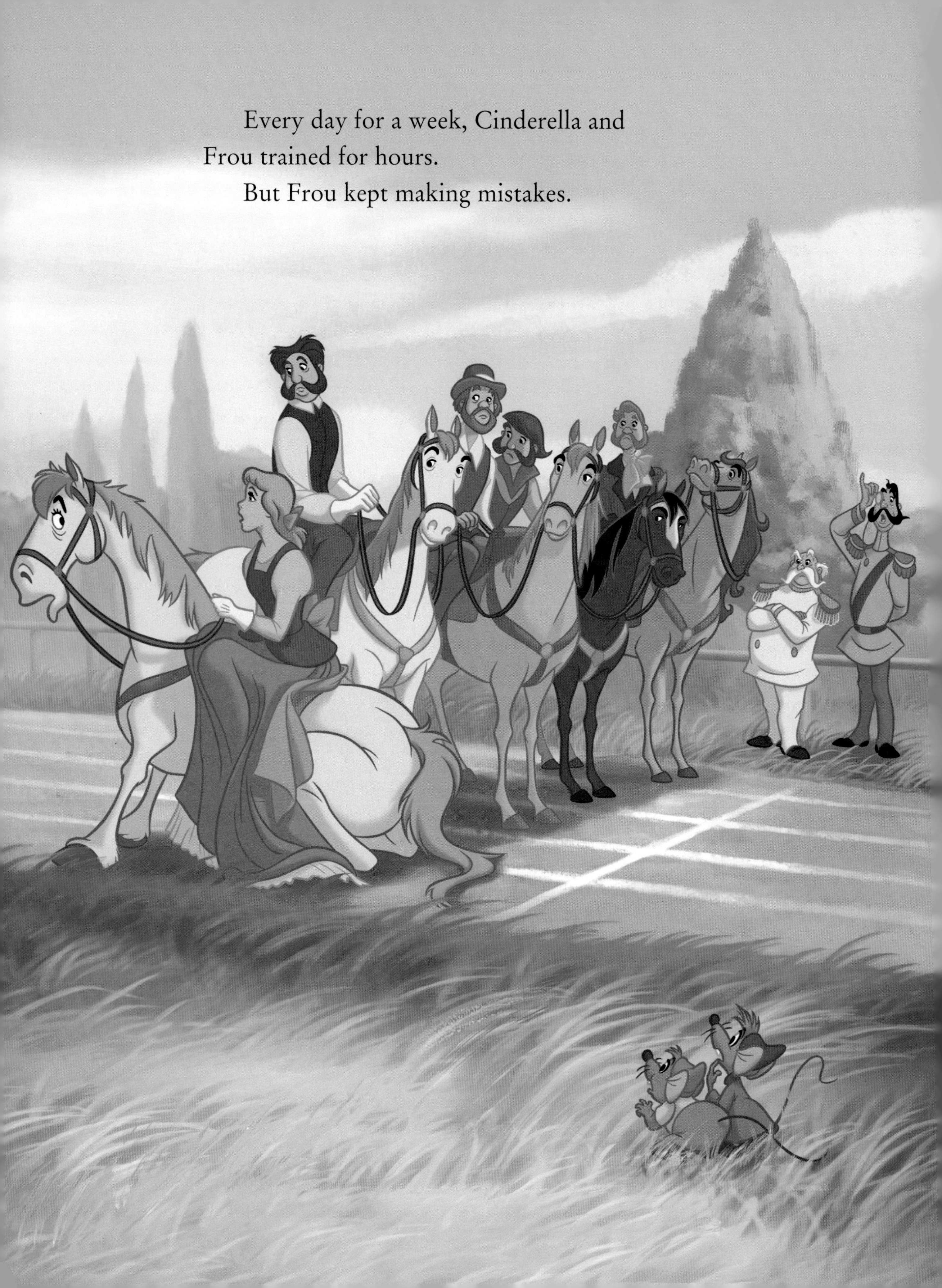

Every day for a week, Cinderella and Frou trained for hours.

But Frou kept making mistakes.

No matter how sweetly Cinderella urged him, he missed every jump.

And no matter how firmly she steered him, he took the wrong turn every time.

"Oh, Frou," Cinderella said, patting his shaggy head, "I know you can do it!"

But no one else was quite so sure—especially not Frou!

At last, it was the night before the royal horse show.

"Please don't worry," Cinderella told Frou. "You're going to be wonderful. Tomorrow will be fun!"

But Frou didn't seem to believe her.

"Did someone say 'fun'?" a voice asked. Cinderella turned around. It was her fairy godmother!

“I overheard your little mouse friends talking,” she explained. “They said you need a miracle. So, here I am!”

Cinderella laughed and shook her head. “Oh, that’s kind of you,” she said. “But we don’t need a miracle, just a good night’s sleep.”

"My dear," her fairy godmother whispered, "*you* know Frou can win, and *I* know Frou can win, but our friend Frou doesn't know it at all. What he needs is a reason to feel confident."

And with that, she raised her magic wand and waved it at Frou. To Frou's amazement, a glass horseshoe appeared on each of his hooves!

"With these horseshoes, you'll never miss a step," she told Frou, sneaking a wink at Cinderella. "And while I'm at it," she added, "Bibbidi-Bobbidi-Boo!" She waved her wand again. Instantly, a golden saddle appeared on Frou's back, and Cinderella's simple dress became a beautiful riding habit.

"How can we ever thank you?" asked Cinderella.

"As you said," replied her fairy godmother, "just have fun!"

The next day at the horse show, Cinderella saw more fine horses than she ever had before. They all looked like champions—but so did Frou! He held his head up high and stamped his hooves proudly. The King himself could hardly believe that Frou was the same horse he'd been watching trip and stumble all week long.

Frou cleared every jump with ease and never took an awkward step or a wrong turn. He even managed a graceful little bow at the end. And it was all thanks to the magical glass horseshoes—or so Frou thought.

Cinderella knew better, though. The glass horseshoes just gave Frou the confidence he needed in order to be the great horse he always had been.

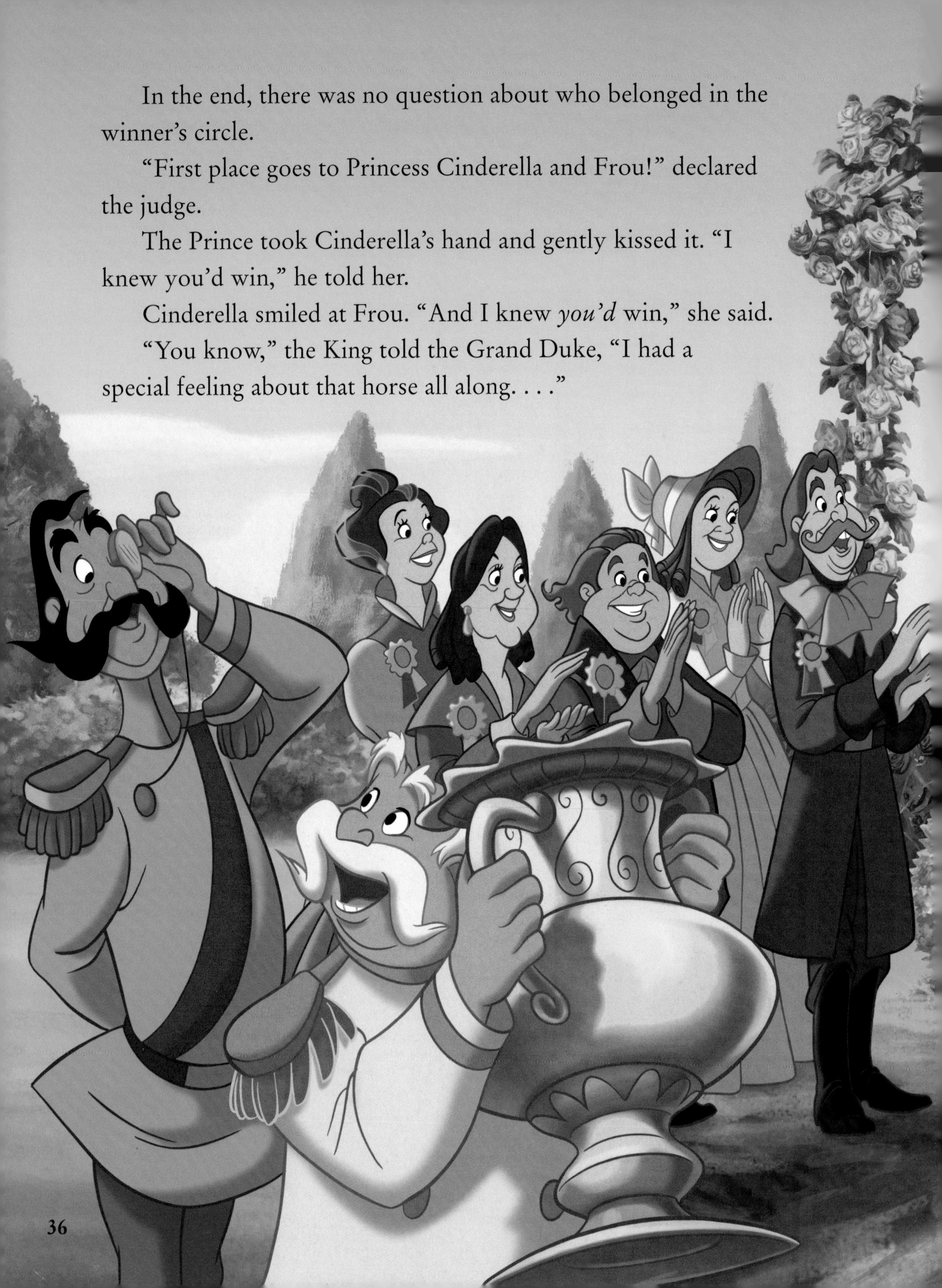

In the end, there was no question about who belonged in the winner's circle.

"First place goes to Princess Cinderella and Frou!" declared the judge.

The Prince took Cinderella's hand and gently kissed it. "I knew you'd win," he told her.

Cinderella smiled at Frou. "And I knew *you'd* win," she said.

"You know," the King told the Grand Duke, "I had a special feeling about that horse all along. . . ."

1st

After the horse show, Frou returned to his stall at the palace stable, with his head a little higher, his back a little straighter, and his glass shoes at the ready for the next time duty called.

Walt Disney's

Snow White and the Seven Dwarfs

To the Rescue!

Snow White and her prince spent nearly every day together. But one particularly sunny morning, the Prince told Snow White that he had an important errand to take care of. "I will be away for several hours, I'm afraid," he said.

"I'll miss you," said Snow White. She herself was planning on spending the day in the palace gardens.

Snow White changed her dress and set about her gardening. The Prince saddled his trusty steed, Astor, and rode to the garden to bid Snow White farewell.

"Take good care of my prince," Snow White said, slipping a flower into Astor's bridle.

Then she gave one to the Prince. "And take good care of Astor!" she said. (For Snow White loved the faithful horse, too.) She smiled and waved as she watched them trot off down the road.

The time flew by. Before long, Snow White looked up from the roses she was tending and saw a cloud of dust on the road. A horse was rapidly approaching.

"Oh, good!" she exclaimed, clapping her hands together. "The Prince and Astor are home early!"

Brushing the dirt from her clothes, she hurried toward the gate to greet them as they arrived.

Imagine Snow White's surprise when she saw that Astor was alone! The princess looked from Astor's empty saddle to the now quiet road.

"Why, where's the Prince?" she wondered out loud.

But only Astor knew the answer, and, of course, the horse couldn't say.

Snow White tried not to panic. But her tender heart quickly filled with dread.

Surely the Prince is in some sort of trouble, she thought. Why else would Astor return to the palace without him?

"I must go and find him!" she declared bravely. And without wasting another moment, she grabbed her cloak and started down the road.

Suddenly, Snow White felt a warm breath on the back of her neck. She turned—and there was Astor.

"What is it?" she asked.

The horse stamped her hoof on the ground and nodded toward her empty saddle.

"Do you want me to get on?" Snow White asked.

Again, Astor nodded.

Goodness! thought Snow White. *Maybe she can tell me where the Prince is, after all!* Quickly, the princess pulled herself into the saddle. She barely had time to sit down before Astor was racing down the road toward the forest!

Astor ran deeper and deeper into the woods with Snow White tugging uselessly at the reins. The princess tried not to think about what dangers might await them on the dark path ahead.

If only she knew where Astor was taking her.

If only she knew that the Prince was safe!

Tirelessly, Astor galloped through the woods. She darted between trees and leaped over briars and brambles.

Then, suddenly, Snow White spotted a piece of red cloth caught on a long, sharp thorn.

A knot formed in her throat. Could it be? It was! A scrap torn from the Prince's very own riding cloak!

And that wasn't all! As she ducked beneath a low-hanging branch, Snow White glimpsed a spot of red on the muddy ground. There was no mistaking those deep crimson petals. They were from the very rose Snow White had given the Prince that morning!

She tugged on Astor's reins, begging the horse to stop. But Astor charged ahead, and Snow White had no choice but to go along.

At last, they reached the river. Surely Astor will have to stop here, Snow White thought. But the pace only quickened. Indeed, it was soon clear to Snow White that Astor planned to jump across the river!

Just then, Snow White saw the Prince's feathered hat dangling from a limb high above the water.

There was no time to think. As Astor leaped across the river, Snow White reached up as high as she could . . . and plucked the hat from the branch.

Snow White gripped Astor's reins with one hand. With the other, she clutched the Prince's hat to her chest. She could only imagine the horrible danger her dear, sweet prince was in.

Her thoughts were soon interrupted by a startling noise.

Four eyes glared at her from the shadows ahead.

"Oh!" Snow White cried. Astor bravely reared up to defend her.

"Well, tello hair . . . I mean, *hello there*!" said a familiar voice.

"Doc?" Snow White said, with a sigh of relief. "I'm so very glad to see you!"

"Likewise, my dear. But what's the matter?" Doc asked, surprised to see the princess looking so upset.

"It's the Prince," Snow White said, showing him the crumpled hat. "I have to find him!"

"Don't worry, Princess," Doc assured her. "We can help you!"

Doc put his fingers to his lips and whistled. Within seconds, the other Dwarfs arrived.

"The Prince is missin'," Doc explained to the Dwarfs. "And we're gonna help Snow White find him!"

"Let's . . . let's . . . let's—*achoo!*—let's go!" Sneezy cried.

"Oh, thank you," Snow White said as Astor impatiently stamped her hooves. "Just follow Astor," she added. "She seems to know the way."

The Seven Dwarfs and their ponies followed Snow White and Astor through the depths of the forest and over a deep, rocky canyon.

"Ooh," said Bashful, looking down. "I hope the Prince isn't down there."

"Shh!" Grumpy growled back at him. "You'll scare the princess."

But Snow White had heard. She clutched the Prince's hat and concentrated on thinking hopeful thoughts.

Finally, they emerged into a sunny clearing, and Astor slowed to a stop. Snow White blinked in the bright light and then spotted the Prince, lying on the ground. "Oh, no!" she cried.

Astor knelt down slightly so the princess could slip out of the saddle. The faithful horse whinnied as Snow White ran to the Prince's side.

"Don't worry!" Snow White called to the Prince as she raced across the clearing. "I'm coming!"

Breathless, Snow White reached the Prince just as he sat up and stretched. "What a nice nap!" he said. "And what a lovely way to awake. I hope you're hungry!"

Snow White was bewildered. Next to the Prince lay a lavish picnic spread out on a soft blanket. And the Prince was as happy and healthy as ever!

"I knew Astor would get you here quickly," he said, beaming. "Tell me. Are you surprised?"

Snow White paused for a moment to catch her breath.

"Oh, yes, very surprised," she said at last, smiling.

The Prince looked amused as the Seven Dwarfs began digging into the delicious food.

"Well," he said with a laugh, "I'm glad I brought a little extra."

"Me, too," Snow White replied. She picked up an apple and offered it to Astor.

"And," she added, "I'm *very* glad you have such a dear and clever horse!"

Disney's

Beauty and the Beast

A Friend for Phillipe

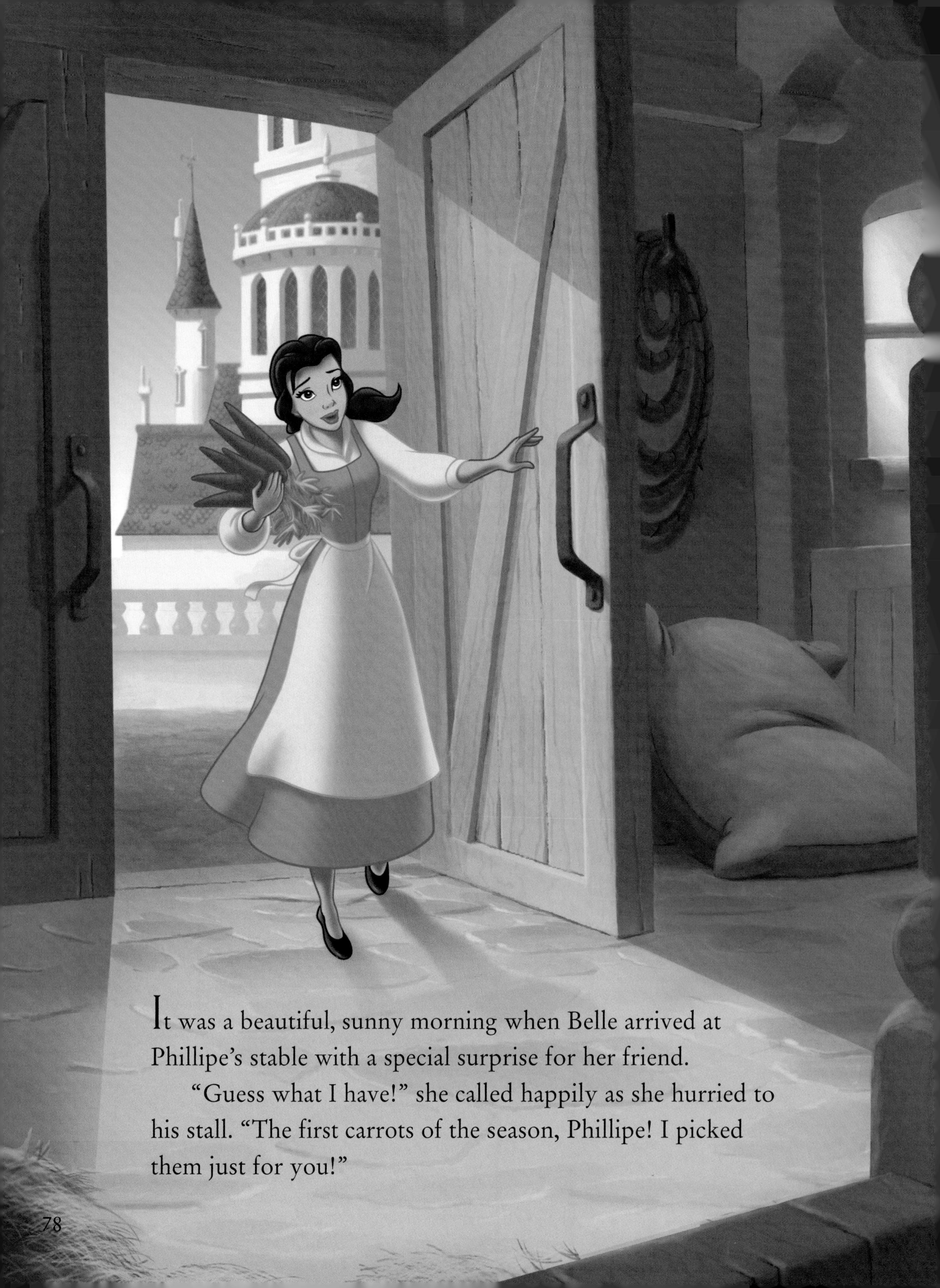

It was a beautiful, sunny morning when Belle arrived at Phillipe's stable with a special surprise for her friend.

"Guess what I have!" she called happily as she hurried to his stall. "The first carrots of the season, Phillipe! I picked them just for you!"

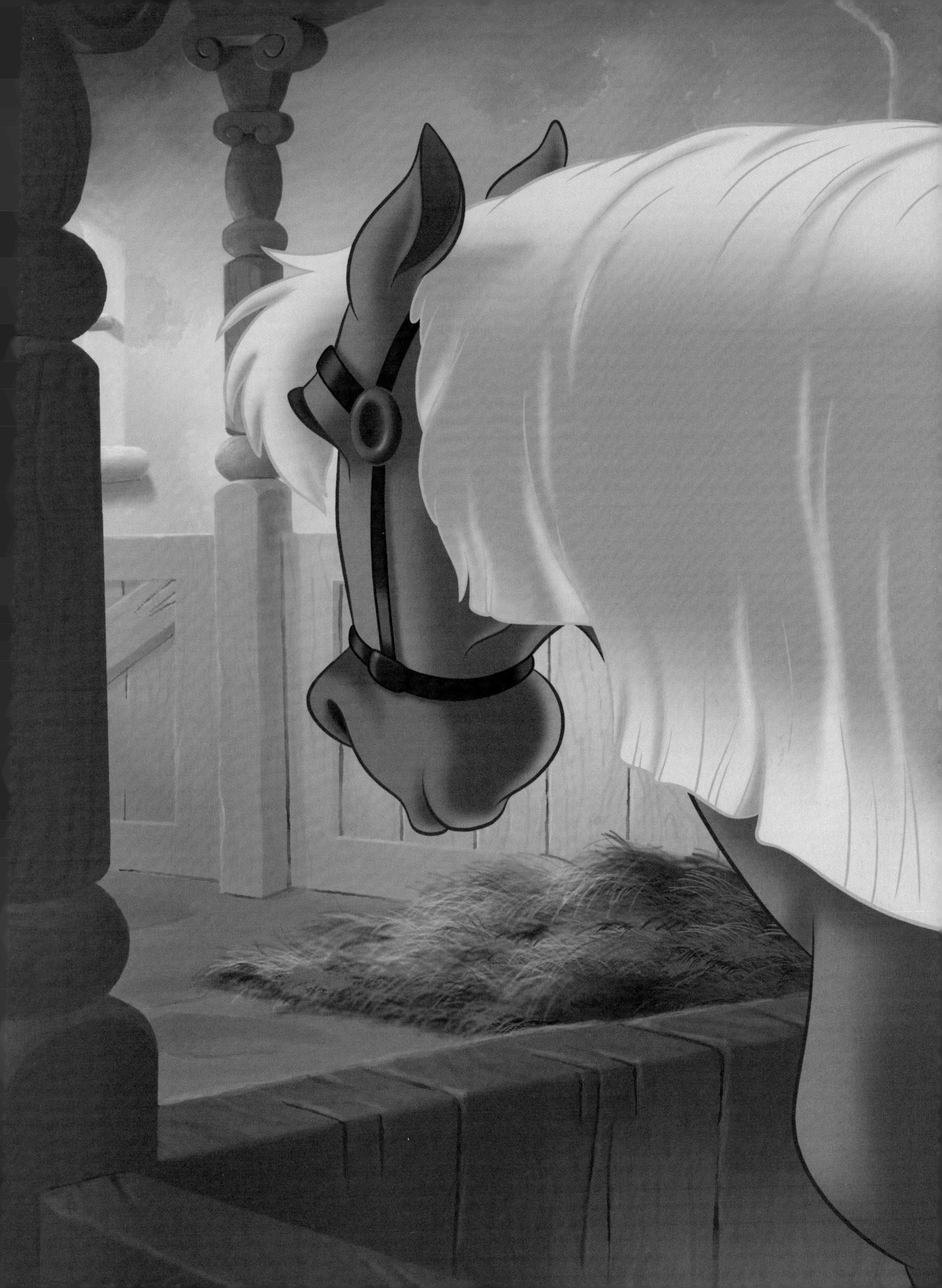

Phillipe was not as happy as Belle had hoped he would be. He sniffed at the bunch of carrots. But when Belle offered him one, Phillipe gently butted her hands away.

"Is something wrong?" Belle asked, alarmed. Phillipe was *always* hungry.

Phillipe hung his head and sighed a little sigh. There was something wrong, all right, Belle thought. Phillipe was the gloomiest horse she had ever seen!

Belle decided that she simply *had* to cheer up Phillipe. But how?

"If only you could talk," Belle said to Phillipe, "you could tell me *exactly* what to do." But he couldn't, so Belle would have to figure it out on her own. She hurried to the library and gathered all the books about horses she could find. Then she sat down to read every single one of them.

Horses
Who Love Oats
Too Much
Carrot Soup
for the
Horse's Soul
MACRAME
YOUR OWN SADDLE

"*Sacre bleu!*" cried Lumiere when he, Cogsworth, and Chip saw all the books. "What are you doing, Princess?"

"I want to cheer up Phillipe," Belle explained. "I hoped I'd find the answer in one of these books . . . but I'm not having much luck."

"Ah!" said Lumiere, "before you came and freed us from the enchantment, we were often sad."

"But," the former candelabrum remembered, "we always found ways to cheer ourselves up. You must brighten his stall! It's important to have the right *atmosphere*, you know!"

"I do believe that *music* is the key to happiness," Cogsworth said. "It always made me smile when I was an enchanted clock."

"Or how about a bubble bath?" Chip chimed in. "That used to cheer me up!"

Belle decided to give each idea a try.

First, she helped Lumiere brighten up Phillipe's stall. They covered the walls with wallpaper and trimmed them with gold. They piled pillows in the corners, hung curtains in the windows, and filled the room with flowers. And for the final brightening touch, they hung a huge chandelier from the ceiling.

"Voilà!" Lumiere exclaimed. "What more could a horse ask for?"

Phillipe stared sadly out the window.

"I wish I knew," said Belle.

Next, Cogsworth set up an orchestra in the stable. Belle, Lumiere, and Chip listened politely as Cogsworth led the musicians through a very, *very* long concert.

Phillipe didn't seem to enjoy the concert much at all. But at least, Belle thought brightly, his appetite has returned!

Finally, Belle saw to it that Phillipe was treated to a bubble bath fit for a king.

"If this doesn't make him smile," Belle told Chip, "I don't know *what* will!"

But in the end, though he was shiny and sweet-smelling, Phillipe was just as glum—and Belle was just as puzzled.

"Maybe the Prince will know what to do," Chip suggested.

Belle thought this was an excellent idea. She found the Prince in his study and explained everything to him. "I wish I knew what Phillipe needed!" she cried. "Do you have any suggestions?"

The Prince thought for a moment. "Maybe a walk would do him good," he said. "A good walk always used to cheer me up."

"Of course!" Belle agreed. "That's a wonderful idea!"

Quickly, Belle changed into her riding clothes and hurried to fetch Phillipe's saddle. When he saw her coming, he perked right up.

"Silly me! What was I thinking?" Belle said as she saddled him. "You'd *really* like a nice ramble, wouldn't you?"

Belle led Phillipe to the edge of the forest where the royal orchards began. The sight of all of the delicious fruit gave Belle an idea.

"Would you like an apple?" Belle asked. "Go ahead and choose one!"

Following Belle's suggestion, Phillipe wandered from tree to tree, eyeing each apple and even sniffing some. But soon his head was hanging, and his steps were slow and heavy. It was clear his heart wasn't in it.

Still, Belle did not give up. They continued on to a wide, open meadow.

"You know," Belle said, "I bet a good gallop would do the trick." She leaned forward and snapped the reins, giving Phillipe's sides a firm nudge with her heels.

As if to tell her, "Wrong again," Phillipe stopped, leaned down, and nibbled at the clover.

"Oh, Phillipe," Belle said in despair. "I just don't know what else to do!"

Then, all of a sudden, Phillipe's ears pricked up, and his head snapped to attention. Belle barely had time to sit up before Phillipe charged off like a racehorse out of the gate!

"Whoa, boy!" Belle cried, nearly falling out of the saddle. "Phillipe! Where are you going?"

But Phillipe just charged on, straight into the forest.

At last they emerged from the trees . . . into a clearing filled with wild, beautiful horses! Belle and Phillipe stared at the herd before them. Then Phillipe whinnied, and several of the wild horses answered him.

Finally, Belle realized what Phillipe had wanted. Not a fancy stall, or fine music, or a bubble bath. Not an apple or a run. What Phillipe had wanted was to be with other *horses*!

"Well, go on," Belle said as she swung out of the saddle. "Go have some fun!"

She didn't have to tell him twice. Phillipe trotted eagerly over to the herd.

All afternoon, Belle watched Phillipe race and play. Soon, he had even made a friend! The two horses grazed, chased each other around the clearing, and dozed together in the warm sun.

All too quickly, the day was over, and the sun began to set. "Oh, goodness!" cried Belle. "We've got to get going!"

So she put Phillipe's saddle on and they started back toward the castle. "I promise we'll come back soon!" Belle told Phillipe.

As they made their way through the meadow, Belle found herself wishing Phillipe had a horse friend at the castle. "If only there was a way—" Belle began.

She was interrupted by the sound of hooves behind them. Belle turned around.

"Well, look at that, Phillipe!" she exclaimed. "It's your new friend."

The horse who had played with Phillipe all afternoon was following them home.

Belle and Phillipe slowed their pace, and the shy horse drew closer . . .

. . . and closer.

By the time they reached the castle, the two horses were walking side by side.

"Welcome to our castle!" Belle told the new horse when they arrived. "We're honored to have you as our guest!"

And to show the horse she meant it, Belle hurried to fix up the stall next to Phillipe's.

"There," she said when she was through. "Now *this* looks like a stable where a horse (or two!) could really live happily ever after!"

And that is exactly what they did.